Little Rabbit's Big

Charlotte van Emst

RED FOX

For Raymond

And thank you to Hannah
for a big day in the park

A Red Fox Book

Published by Random Century Children's Books
20 Vauxhall Bridge Road, London SW1V 2SA
A division of the Random Century Group

London Melbourne Sydney Auckland
Johannesburg and agencies throughout the world

First published in Great Britain by
Hutchinson Children's Books 1989

Red Fox edition 1991

Copyright © Charlotte van Emst 1989

The right of Charlotte van Emst to be identified as the
author of this work has been asserted by her in accordance
with the Copyright, Designs and Patents Act, 1988.

Printed in Singapore

ISBN 0-09-966880-7

It was a big day for Little Rabbit. He was going to the park with Bear.

'Be good,' said Mum as she waved goodbye, 'you're a big
rabbit now.'

'Remember, Bear,' said Little Rabbit, on the way to the park,
'I'm not little today. I'm *big*!'

'In fact, I'll soon be too big for this pushchair.'

The moment they arrived, Little Rabbit rushed straight for
the swings.
    'Look at me!' he cried. 'Big rabbits can swing *really* high.'

Back and forth and up and down he went, higher and
higher . . .
and higher . . .
and higher . . .
and HIGHER.

'Whoops!'

When Bear looked round, Little Rabbit was already halfway
up the slide.

'Look at me!' he shouted. 'No hands!'

'Wheeeee!'

BUMP!

But Little Rabbit was determined to be big and brave.
'Let's play hide-and-seek,' he said.

Bear found a good hiding place. Little Rabbit looked over here and over there; under this and under that. He couldn't find Bear anywhere.

'Where are you?' he sniffed.

'Over here!' cried Bear, jumping out from behind a tree.
'I've found *you*.'
    But big, bold rabbits never stay miserable for long . . . .

On the way to the duck pond they watched the Teddy Rovers practising for Saturday's big match. 'I'll show you how to play football,' yelled Little Rabbit. 'Just watch me!'

Little Rabbit gave the ball a huge kick . . . .

'Ouch!'

'Well done,' said the big centre forward. Little Rabbit felt very proud, even though his toe hurt quite a lot.

At last they reached the duck pond. 'Those ducks look
hungry,' said Little Rabbit. 'See how far I can throw.'

The bread went soaring through the air . . .

. . . and so did Little Rabbit.

SPLASH!

'That was a *huge* throw,' said Bear, helping him out.

'I'll jump myself dry,' suggested Little Rabbit. 'I'm good at jumping.'

But the mud was all slippery . . . .

'Never mind,' said Bear. 'Let's have an ice cream.'

Little Rabbit chose a treble decker strawberry whizz with a chocolate flake. 'Big rabbits need really big ice creams,' he said.

'And we can eat them all in one go!'

'I think it's time we went home,' said Bear. 'It's been a big day.'

Back at home, Little Rabbit began to feel small again. He let
Bear run his bath.

He let her rinse his face when he got soap in his eyes.

'Don't worry, you'll soon feel better,' said Bear, as she
wrapped him up in a nice warm towel.

Little Rabbit hoped so!

Later on, Bear was busy in the kitchen. 'There's a surprise for tea,' she said.

Little Rabbit was glad he was small enough for special
surprises . . .

. . . like chocolate cake.

He was glad he was small enough for it not to matter too
much . . .

. . . if he made a mess.

He was glad he was small enough to be carried upstairs . . .

. . . and cuddled

and read a story

and tucked up tight . . .

. . . and kissed goodnight.

I'm glad I'm not *always* a big rabbit, he thought as he closed his eyes.

But one day . . . .

THE END